The Kingdom Of

To,
My loving and affectionate parents

For information contact:
Yahvi Mehta
Yahvi12@outlook.com

Book and Cover design by Designer: Yahvi
ISBN:

First Edition: December 2024

Acknowledgement

It's often said that weaving a story is simple, capturing it on paper can be quite a challenge. I owe my ability to undertake this journey to the unwavering encouragement of my mother, Mrs. Anamika Mehta, whose belief in me was a beacon of light. Many individuals played pivotal roles in helping me shape this book into something truly special. I am deeply grateful to my teacher, Ms. Pallavi Saha, who has been my guiding star throughout this writing adventure. Her support not only helped me hone my skills but also opened my mind to new possibilities.

I cannot forget the love and encouragement from my father, Mr. Kapil Mehta and younger brother, Havish, who inspired me with their genuine interest every time I shared my stories with them. I have always found comfort in the works of authors like Roald Dahl, J.K. Rowling, Enid Blyton, Conan Doyle, Agatha Christie, and Chitra Banerjee Divakaruni. Their creative narratives are not just tales but windows into unique worlds that captivate the imagination. I also want to extend my heartfelt thanks to all my wonderful school teachers, whose encouragement has nurtured my passion and pushed me to explore my potentials.

About the Author

At just 13 years old, Yahvi Mehta is an inquisitive and imaginative young author who delights in crafting stories that explore the realms of adventure, mystery, and horror. Despite her busy schedule, which leaves her with limited free time, Yahvi is committed to making the most of her leisure hours by engaging in intellectually stimulating activities. She especially enjoys creating intricate portraits and realistic artworks that showcase her art. Yahvi possesses a deep-seated connection with nature, which plays a significant role in her writing. She often finds inspiration in the beauty and complexity of the natural world, believing that it can captivate her readers' imaginations.

Character Page

Leena
'The Protagonist'

Ms.Azura
'The Head of the Kingdom'

Roommates

Suzan

Daniel

Tofu

Evils

Hadarki

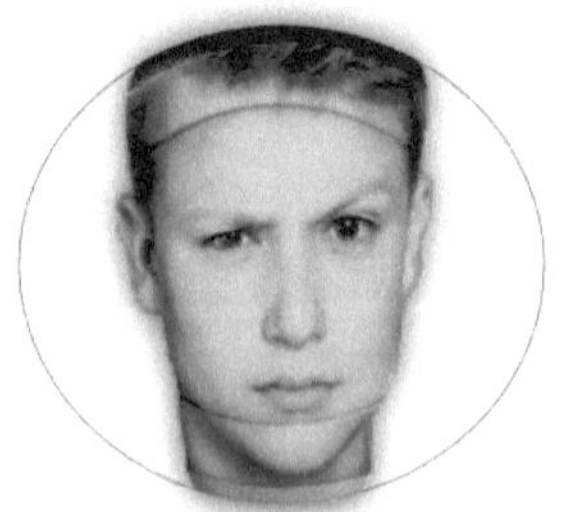

Ben

Index

Contents Pg.no

Chapter 1 8

Chapter 2 14

Chapter 3 22

Chapter 4 27

Chapter 5 33

Chapter 6 38

Chapter 7 43

Chapter 8 48

Chapter 9 51

Chapter 10 55

Chapter 11 60

Chapter 12 64

Chapter 13 69

Chapter 14 73

Chapter 15 78

A serene village, El Vergel, is nestled deep within the lush, verdant foliage of the Amazon rainforest. Everyone visited the village square, the heart of the village, in the evening. Thus, feeling the air with chatter and happiness. In the distance, the majestic Amazon River meandered through the thick rainforest, with its turquoise water reflecting the blue sky above and its clear blue waters teeming with fish and other aquatic life.

Leena, a young indigenous girl not more than 15 years old, lived with her loving parents in this village. She slogged for hours in the field, helping her family. Despite the long hours of work, Leena remained a gracious figure with a warm smile. She was a girl of few words, but her eyes spoke volumes. Her long, dark hair cascaded down her back like a gentle waterfall, and her skin was honey-coloured. She wore a simple dress made of cotton, which she wove herself, a shining purple locket, and her feet were bare.

Leena's day started early, long before the sun rose. She woke up to the sound of birds chirping and the distant roar of the jungle. She lived in a small cottage made of bamboo and a thatched roof, surrounded by a small garden where her family grew vegetables and fruits. Her house was a blend of modern and old styles, and she could see the crystal-clear Amazon River from her house.

Her parents were hardworking people who had instilled in her the values of hard work, honesty, and kindness and her day ended in the early evening.

Early morning while Leena was cleaning the attic, she came across a weathered diary of her grandmother. With a sense of curiosity overcoming her, she cautiously opened the pages and began to peruse the contents. As she reached the very end, her eyes came upon a startling declaration that read, "Leena is not an ordinary person. The powers in her control will help the kingdom - Heir of the Elysium." This statement left her feeling both perplexed and captivated, and she fumbled to hold onto the book amidst her excitement. With an urgent need to understand more about the kingdom of Elysium and the powers mentioned in the diary, she hastily ran to her mother for answers.

Puffing out heavily, she questioned her mother about the same. 'Darling, even I have no clue about it. Come on, now leave it and quickly go back to work,' replied her mother. She was not at all satisfied with her words, but to an extent, she might be right.

The next day, the first signs of spring appeared. Leena eagerly began planting seeds in the rich soil, readying herself for the next harvest. The warm afternoon sun radiated its golden light upon her face. Leena's eyes got a glimpse of something sparkling in the river. She ran rashly towards it. What a surprise! A massive fish broke the surface, revealing its iridescent scales that shimmered like diamonds and its powerful tail that propelled it through the water with ease. Leena was utterly captivated by the sheer majesty of the fish as it played.

She quickly jumped into the water to follow this magnificent fish. The fish seemed to be leading her on a wondrous journey, darting ahead before stopping to wait for her, its movements almost playful. Leena's heart raced with excitement and anticipation, her lungs burning as she struggled to hold her breath. She followed the fish deeper into the mysterious underwater world, unsure of what lay ahead but driven by an unyielding curiosity and a deep sense of attraction. The ocean floor was a mesmerizing kaleidoscope of vibrant colours and intricate shapes, with schools of fish swimming past in every direction, creating a spectacular display of nature's beauty.

As she submerged deeper into the river, the locket released its magical powers, transforming her into a stunning mermaid. Her arms and legs morphed into a graceful fishtail, adorned with colorful scales of various shades of blue and green. Her hair flowed freely behind her, swaying like seaweed as she swam effortlessly through the water. She was astonished to see the magic of her locket. She swam deeper into the mysterious depths, eager to explore the secrets that lay hidden beneath the surface.

Chapter 2

Leena dived into the ocean with a graceful plunge, her body slicing through the water easily. The surrounding school of fish and vibrant corals provided a breathtaking view. As she swam, her eyes caught a glimpse of something peculiar - a massive vortex of water and debris, swirling ferociously like a tornado beneath the surface. Despite her efforts to swim away from it, the powerful force of the vortex pulled her in, causing her to spin and twirl uncontrollably.

As she emerged from the violent vortex that had swallowed her while she was swimming, she found herself standing in a place that was entirely different from what she had expected. As she rubbed her eyes to clear her vision, she was stunned by the overwhelming beauty of the surroundings that greeted her. The place was like nothing she had ever seen before. Before her, lay a hidden city, the towering buildings were exquisite. The buildings were constructed with pearls and jewels. Covered by the creepers they encircled a humungous kingdom in amidst.

As she went a few miles she could see a magnificent castle adorned with colourful banners, their designs depicting the coat of arms of the kingdom she had just entered. The palace itself was a wonder to behold – a lavish masterpiece of architecture. The intricate details and the magnificent structure of the palace left her in awe.

The butterflies hovering around were shining, and the fruity aroma of flowers was magnificent, the whole scene was like something out of a fairy tale, leaving her stunned.

As she gazed upon the splendour before her, she couldn't help but wonder what secrets lay hidden within this mysterious place. She felt an overwhelming urge to explore this magnificent city.

"Good morning, ladies and Gentlemen, you are requested to assemble in front of the palace within half an hour." Came an echoing sound. Leena looked around to see where the sound was coming from. Her eyes had spotted an old woman with short blond hair and a firm body who stood on the castle platform. Her voice boomed like a roaring lion which had made everyone all ears.

After half an hour, Leena and the crowd of people present there cursorily assembled.

The woman addressed to everyone 'I, the head of this city, Azura has a great honour to welcome you. This is the Kingdom of Elysium; you all have been chosen for your capabilities and hierarchy. At 10 Am you must arrive at the hall inside the kingdom '.

As Leena sat there, her mind was in a state of utter confusion and disarray. The reason? She had just stumbled upon a peculiar phrase in her grandmother's diary - "Kingdom of Elysium". It was as if this one phrase had the power to unravel the very fabric of her being and reveal her true destiny. The weight of this discovery was almost overwhelming, and she couldn't help but wonder what it all meant.

A group of peculiar little elves were bustling in the vast kingdom. One of them, who was setting a table, excitedly exclaimed, "Hey there, Bonjour! Madame!" Leena too said 'Salut! Il fait beau.' The elf realized she knew French and quickly replied, 'Oui.' Later, the grand clock tower located in the heart of the castle let out a deafening chime, echoing throughout the kingdom.

'Greetings! The long-awaited moment has finally arrived, and we are pleased to inform you that we have assigned rooms for your comfortable stay. You will be accompanied by our diligent helpers, the elves, who will guide you to your respective rooms. We urge you to take some rest and get acquainted with your roommate, who might become your friend in this fascinating kingdom. You are free to explore and discover the wonders of this realm. Your teaching sessions will commence from tomorrow, and we kindly request you to join us in the dining room at 8 pm for dinner. We will share further instructions with you during the meal. We hope you have a pleasant stay here.'

Addressed Azura.

As she stepped foot in the new place, the picture was still a bit hazy to her. However, she knew she had to go with the flow and make the most of it. Without wasting any time, she was allocated a room with three roommates - a girl named Suzan and two boys named Tofu and Daniel. To her surprise, they all got along pretty well from the get-go. As Leena and Suzan were setting up their room, they stumbled upon an old book called "The Mysteries." The book looked quite intriguing.

As they turned the pages of the book, their eyes fell upon the image of a magnificent female warrior named Dasha. The illustration depicted her as a powerful and fearless fighter who had once saved the entire kingdom from a horrifying and catastrophic event. Alongside her stood a majestic and graceful butterfly, adding enchantment and wonder to the already captivating scene.

It was already dinner time; they didn't even notice when the time flew. The start of dinner was amazing. The elves invited them through a poem which goes like this: -

Welcome to the grand castle's gate,
Where ancient secrets whisper and legends await.
The gems, like radiant stars, hold our might,
A treasure trove of power, gleaming so bright.
Just like nectar for a magical flight,
They fuel our kingdom with wondrous light.

As you step into this splendid scene,
You'll find students in awe, living a dream.
The grandeur of this place, so vast,
Will fill you with wonder and fill you with pride.
You'll be amazed to discover why,
Some arrived here by fish or butterfly.
And a few were brought by a dwarf's flight,
Each arrival is a marvel, a breathtaking sight.

Letters to your parents have taken flight,
To inform them of your extraordinary stay,
In this kingdom of light, keeping darkness at bay,
A haven of safety, come what may.

'Welcome to your destiny. It's been nice meeting you. Tomorrow morning, at 6 am, you have to gather in the backyard for your first lesson. Now chuck in everyone.' Exclaimed Ms.Azura.

The table was draped with white cloth on top of that rested beautiful golden plates and the dishes were numerous but tasty. What not was there, each variety staring from stater to the desert was prepared. The air in the hall filled with chatter and whispers of students. All were having a pleasant time.

Chapter 3

Leena, Suzan, Daniel, and Tofu made their way back to their respective dormitories. They recounted their recent travel experiences with each other. The living room where they convened was a picture of comfort and soft lighting that cast a warm, inviting glow. The crackling fireplace added a touch of cosiness, enveloping the room in a comforting essence as the friends settled in to share their adventures.

After hearing the amazing tale of Suzan and Tofu arriving on a giant butterfly and Daniel being brought by a quirky little dwarf, Leena too said her side of the story. they establish a strong rapport with each other. They had put on their night suit and slept early as they didn't want to get late for their first lesson.

At 5 a.m., the colossal clock in the grand hall

reverberated with a resounding chime that echoed throughout the entire kingdom, rousing the students from their slumber. Startled by the echoing sound that sent shivers down their spine, Leena jolted awake.

On the exciting first day of school, they took their showers and dashed out to the backyard. They released a sigh of relief as they saw teachers in sight. The air was abuzz with chatter. Everyone got a grip on themselves for what awaited them next.

After a period of waiting, Ms. Azura made her entrance with a lady who confidently boasted a firm, athletic physique and short hair that elegantly curled and framed her shoulders. Her strong and self-assured presence commanded our attention.

'So, Children you might be dreaming of this place and what are the capabilities in you that brought you here? Many of your grandparents were part of the kingdom so their qualities might have been inculcated in you or you might have certain qualities of leadership and that of a warrior. The castle was set free by your grandparents in 1701. They protected the kingdom from the dark magic of the evil witch, Hadarki. You are our future guardian. I hope you to be trained to protect the kingdom from further attacks.'

'I'm delighted to introduce Ms. Nonna to the class. She is going to be your instructor in animal care. 'Everyone cheered as they greet her. 'Children, let's do something interesting today. The ball in the elf's hand can let you all choose a butterfly that matches your type. The crystal ball will glow if you can establish a link with them. Make sure you dare not cross the fence; the butterflies are in the forest behind you. I'm positive that every instruction is understood. In addition, you have an hour to select your butterfly and deliver it to this location. You will be returned to your homes if you don't.' told Ms Nonna

"On your marks, ready, set!" declared Ms Azura

Eager to gain their butterflies, everyone ran into the thick woodland. Our next-door roommate's female friend had developed a strong bond with an amazing butterfly. It took Daniel and Tofu fifteen minutes to understand it. Every other student understood it as well. It was just Suzan and Leena. They were both anxious about not receiving any butterflies. Suzan had also formed a bond with a gigantic butterfly after thirty minutes. Leena was the last one left.

When she walked over the fence, she noticed a butterfly that was the prettiest and shiny thing she had ever seen. It declined to bond with Leena's attempts at bonding but was attracted by Leena's locket.

Leena revealed that the locket she was wearing was given to her by her grandmother; at that same time, the crystal shone, and Leena felt a strong emotional connection to it. With renewed determination, Leena and the butterfly raced to join the others at a designated location. Upon their arrival, a collective gasp echoed through the group as they beheld Leena's butterfly in all its radiant glory. Leena heaved a long breath. Its wings shimmered with a mesmerising light, casting a spellbinding aura over everyone present. Everyone was startled at Leena's butterfly from a distance.

'Now, children, notice that each of these creatures has its special characteristics. As soon as you can coordinate with it a special light will illuminate the design that has been created on them. Now you all are requested to pass through the Elysium ring this will select the armour of you and your horse.' Ordered Nonna.

Chapter 4

Wait!" Nonna's sharp voice cut through the air, startling everyone. "Did you just break the rule by crossing the fence?" She pointed a trembling finger at Leena, her gaze piercing. Feeling the weight of Nonna's anger, Leena hesitantly replied, "Yes." Nonna yelled at her "I told you not to go there. Now you are suspended. I noticed the leaf that stuck on you." Gasps filled the air as everyone were taken a back. Nonna's words. Sensing the tension, Azura rushed to the scene and asked, "What happened,

Ms. Nonna?" Nonna, her voice still laced with anger, explained, "This little girl broke the rule on the first day. She crossed the fence and went into the forbidden forest." "Let me talk to her," Azura said in a soothing tone as she gently guided Leena away to the hall.

'Leena, we follow the rules strictly here. You are just like your grandmother, she too did stuff like this. The butterfly that you chose for your companion was your grandmother's companion too,' said Azura staring at Leena's grandmother's idol.

'My grandmother?'

'Yes, she was one of the most powerful guardians who protected our kingdom. She was the only one who had locked the evil woman into the jiffy cave.'

'Is her name-' stumbled Leena

'Valentina' replied Azura instantly.

'Now, I am letting you stay but I don't expect any more breaking of the rules.'

'Yes Ma'am,' said Leena with a relaxed tone.

While returning to the queue of the Elysium ring, Leena wondered about her grandmother as a

great warrior. She speculated about why her grandmother didn't share this secret with her and how she had defeated the evil. She stood last in the line. She saw contestants pass through the Elysium ring and come out with pretty armour on them and the butterfly.

A girl standing just before her, confidently stated, "I will definitely get the fiery red armour." Her attire consisted of tight-fitting jeans, stylish crop tops, and remarkable high heels, and she exuded an almost irritating level of confidence, clearly being proud of her position in the hierarchy.

After passing through the ring, the contestants grouped and talked about their armour. Everyone got an impeccable armour. However, when Leena moved through the ring it was Leena's armour that truly stood out with its flashy appearance, drawing the attention of her peers. Soon they saw Ms. Nonna approaching them to give the next set of instructions.

'Following this, a 3-hour break is scheduled. You are free to return to your dormitories for some rest. You may leave your butterfly here. They would be resting in a butterfly stable down the hill in Butterfly Clenzo.

Moreover, I want to inform you that after the break you are requested to come to the Butterfly Clenzo to learn how to clean their butterfly' declared Ms Nonna.

The triumph of participants stayed relaxed after getting to know about the 3-hour break. They briskly walked to their respective dormitories. After reaching the dormitory Susan continued reading 'The Mysteries'. On the other hand, Tofu and Daniel roamed in the castle to find lots of things. Leena went to get a book from the bookshelf. At that moment Susan read Leena's grandmother's victory in the book, and quickly called Leena to read it. Leena was immensely proud of her grandmother's victory.

After some time, Tofu and Daniel burst into the room and asked Leena and Suzan to show them the top view of Elysium Kingdom through the mighty mountain that guards the castle.

In the evening, they quickly went to the butterfly Clenzo. The elf named Eden was in charge of the cleaning of the butterfly. He taught students how to clean them. Andrew cleaned his butterfly with affection and in this way, he made a bond with the butterfly. In this, the design glowed which looked mesmerising. Sussan messed up all. The bubbles and soap were all over her butterfly segment. Likewise, a few participants messed up and some learnt the art of cleaning perfectly. Leena had fun in cleaning her butterfly with the soap bubble.

The students then went for the dinner. After having dinner Leena alone went to meet her butterfly and sang her the lullaby which she made while eating just for her.

Which goes like this: -

Oh, my butterfly,
You might be tired after flying the whole sky,
I am here, always by your side,
In your dreams, I'll be your guide,
Rest now, in peace
Enjoy a dreamland of colourful trees
Sound sleep
Don't let your dreams seep.

By singing this lullaby, the butterfly went to sleep cosily. She even ensured the elf to take good care of it. She went to her dormitory to get a nice sleep.

The following morning arrived, and the students promptly awoke to the sound of the bell. They quickly dressed, enjoyed breakfast, and sprinted out to the backyard to face the challenge of the day. Nonna awaited them in the centre and greeted them with a cheerful good morning. She then instructed the students to get their butterflies from the Butterfly Clenzo.

As they excitedly received their butterflies, everyone eagerly gathered, wondering about the day's activities. Nonna announced, "Today, we will learn how to fly with our butterflies. The key is to treat them with gentleness and kindness. First, lower your head towards the butterfly; it will reciprocate the gesture. Then, walk gracefully and sit gently on its back. If you follow these steps, it's quite simple. Next, if you sit on it, you might see 4 flowers on its neck. These flowers have arrows marked on them which indicate the directions. Now, I encourage all of you to try the same, but remember, be gentle and considerate with the butterflies."

Daniel's encounter with his butterfly was quite eventful. As he bowed, the butterfly unexpectedly kicked him, adding a touch of unpredictability to their interaction. In contrast, Floria the girl who showed off the most seemed to effortlessly establish a remarkable connection with her butterfly, exuding a sense of confidence and ease in their interaction. Despite initial setbacks, Suzan persevered in her attempts to bond with her butterfly, ultimately finding her rhythm and achieving a harmonious connection. On the other hand, Leena faced notable challenges as her butterfly appeared indifferent to her efforts, proving to be quite unresponsive and stubborn. However, after persistent efforts, she finally managed to gain the butterfly's cooperation and took a ride, marking a significant breakthrough in their relationship.

The speed of Floria on the butterfly was like a thunderbolt. Their harmony was appreciable. After a moment, her butterfly gave a flash of light that symbolised that Floria was the symbol of speed. Likewise, Tofu's butterfly too flashed when they were playing in the water, symbolising that he had the power of water.

Leena, Suzan and Daniel were left to get their power. Everyone enjoyed riding on their butterfly, but Leena didn't because his companion was too lazy.

Leena's butterfly didn't even respond the next consecutive days. The sky was painted black and decorated with shining stars which twinkled high above the sky on the 3rd night. Leena sensed something strange. So, she quickly went with Suzan to the Butterfly Clenzo. When they reached there, they saw that Leena's butterfly was lost. It was not in its stable. She hesitantly asked the elf where it was but he replied casually that he was not aware of it. Leena and Susan scanned the whole castle but it was nowhere to be found.

They then remembered the Wizarding Willow that someone had mentioned. They quickly ran there to ask the wizard to find it through dark magic. There, they were accompanied by Daniel and Tofu who were trying unique magic spells that the wizard taught them. Leena elaborated on the circumstances to the wizard.

The wizard expressed deep sorrow as he shared the unfortunate news. "I regret to inform you that the butterfly you once owned has been captured by an evil witch named Hadarki. With the help of her guardians, she has imprisoned the butterfly in the Jiffy Cave, which is situated in the heart of the forbidden forest. Your grandmother once battled and sealed Hadarki in that very cave."

Leena was shocked at the loss of her butterfly out of her wits. At that very moment Leena, Suzan, Tofu and Daniel rushed toward Azura's bedroom and knocked at the door.

Azura peeped at the door hole and saw them. She instantly opened the door afraid of what would happen to them at late night.

Leena stepped forward and was followed by the others.

Leena exclaimed 'My Butterfly is Lost, Ms.!'

Azura asked quickly 'Are you sure? I don't think so."

Suzan spoke "Yes ma'am it's true. She is nowhere to be found."

Azura deeply said in fear "The darkness is going to fall soon in the Kingdom of Elysium."

Azura quickly went to Nonna's dormitory and signalled her to declare an emergency. Nonna had a loud megaphone through which she informed that students must be there in the dormitory and no one must come out as the castle has been locked for security.

Leena fumbled to ask Ms. Azura about her butterfly. But she asked them to go back to their dormitories instantly.

Chapter 6

In the morning, Leena went to Ms. Azura's dormitory asking her about the situation.

Azura told her that the evil witch named Hadarki had come up with the plan of capturing Elysium again. Leena's grandmother Valentina had fought against her. The battle was truly ferocious.

'What will be her plan this time?' asked Leena.

'I have no clue about the same.' said Azura.

Suzan quickly ran towards Ms.Azura and

promptly asked 'May I know the way to the library?'

'It's on the extreme left of the second floor, my dear.' Suzan rapidly went to the library.

Meanwhile, Azura didn't want to talk about Hadarki as it was a very confidential topic so she said 'I will catch up with you later Leena' and went away.

Leena quickly went to the library where she saw Suzan engrossed in a book. Leena asked Suzan 'Why are you too much into it? Is there something captivating?'

Suzan's eyes lit up as she held the aged book in her hands. Suzan mentioned that it was a magical find from the library - a dusty, weathered book that detailed Hadarki's relentless pursuit to capture the kingdom. The librarian had handed it to her in response to her request for a book about the period when Hadarki tried to capture the castle. As she poured over its pages, she discovered that it contained step-by-step accounts of Hadarki's ambitious conquest. Turning to the last page, she found a cryptic inscription that astounded her and her friend Leena. Leena mentioned finding the same line in her grandmother's diary in her attic.

Intrigued by this unexpected connection, Suzan took the book with her as she and Leena made their way back to their dormitories. They opened both books to see the similarities and differences between them.

In the first book, the symbol on the back page

was identical to the front page of the second book, establishing a mysterious connection between the two. Both books contained a middle page that presented a step-by-step puzzle to solve. Additionally, the first book hinted at the existence of 3 more books following the same intriguing pattern. The clues from the books were:

Clue 1: Find the hidden castle.

Clue 2: Find the original map.

This made Suzan and Leena curious to find more discoveries.

Leena discovered that they had already solved clue 1 by finding the hidden castle 'Elysium'. They have to scam the whole castle to solve the 2nd clue.

The group spared no effort to uncover the long-kept secret. They even took the help of Daniel and Tofu. Suzan scammed through the books in the library. Leena searched in the attic on the other hand Daniel and Tofu chose to read the Volas deeply. This book consisted of hundreds of maps.

Daniel found a similar type of book when he was putting back his wand in the cupboard of wizarding willow.

He opened a book and found a way to reach their goal. Tofu found a hint in the Volas book about where the map might be situated.

He instructed that the map is hidden in room 59. Leena was perplexed about the location of the room. She approached Azura for guidance.

Azura replied 'Students are not allowed to go to room 59.'

Leena hesitantly said, 'It's urgent'.

'But why though?' questioned Azura.

Leena mumbled and went away. A few moments later Daniel passed through Azura's office to go to the backyard then he eavesdropped Ms. Azura and Ms. Nonna. He hurried off towards his friends to tell them about it.

'Don't let the students enter room *59*. It must be strictly restricted as students are on the verge of finding the hidden clues.' Ms. Azura made her instructions crystal clear to Ms. Nonna.

Daniel quickly went to Leena. Seeing Daniel puffing heavily, Leena asked him to calm down and take a deep breath before telling her anything.

He exclaimed 'There is a 90% possibility for the map to be found in room 59!'

Suzan, who was standing beside Leena questioned 'How are you pretty sure about it?'

'Listen, when I was heading towards the backyard, I heard Ms. Azura instructing Ms. Nonna to forbid students from going to room 59. She too mentioned that a clue is hidden there, probably.' said Daniel

Tofu was laser-focused in the Volas book and he finally located room 59. Room 59 was given the symbol.

This symbol suggests that it is a hazardous place.' 💀

Suzan, Leena and Daniel were astonished at the fact and they were pleased at his help.

So, in this way, these four musketeers were able to step another

During dinner time, Ms. Azura seemed certain about the growing curiosity of the 4 musketeers. She announced strolling in school unnecessarily is forbidden.

Gasp filled the hall. But the goal of the four wasn't popped with this pin.

They woke up early in the morning and made strategies to peek into room 59 and get hold of the old map.

They illustrated their strategies in the following picture.

Suzan elaborated the plan that in the evening Daniel would convince Ms. Azura to show her the tricks that he had learnt from the extra classes of Wizarding Willow while Tofu would guide Leena and Suzan to room 59. Then Tofu will be staying out to warn them if in case any teacher is approaching till that time Leena and Suzan will quickly find the map.

After the classes were over they teamed up and cheered Los Uni before the execution of the plan.

Daniel went to Ms. Azura as planned. Ms. Nonna went to the Botany Garden to water her plants. The route to Room 59 was clear. Tofu led the way. When they reached in front of the room they were out of their wits when they spotted an elf guarding it. Fortunately, Suzan was ready with her backup plan. She carried a small play ball to divert the attention of the elf as she had already read that the elves are fond of balls in one of the books in the library, her favourite room.

It worked. Tofu mingled it with a game of catch. Till that time Suzan and Leena entered the room successfully and scanned the place for the 2nd clue-Map.

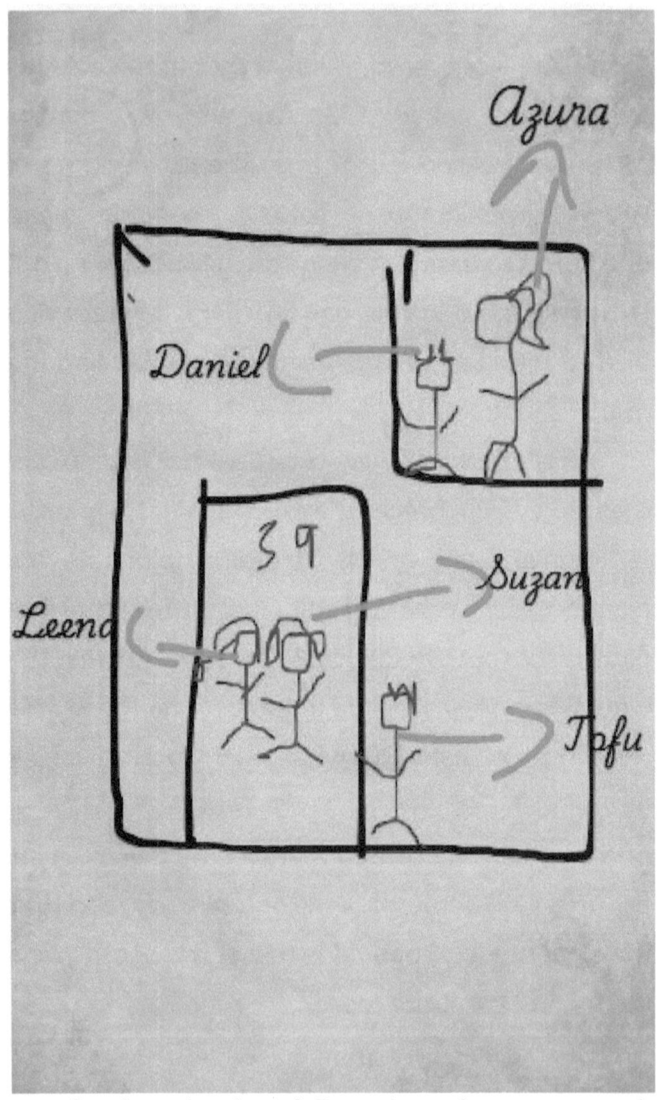

On the other hand, Daniel was having a tough time with Ms. Azura. He had learnt only a few tricks to show. Ms. Azura sensed something aMs. due to his unusual behaviour.

Leena found the map camouflaged with the vintage painting. They took it quickly and ran to their dormitories while Tofu had made the Elf busy. Tofu threw the ball far away and quickly ran.

Unluckily the ball rolled over too far that it landed in Ms. Nonna's botany Garden. Nonna saw the elf playing with the ball in her botany and recognised that he was the guard of room 59. She quickly ran towards the elf and snatched the ball. She scolded him for not being in his position. After a while, she suspected that this ball was given to the elf purposely by the students. She quickly went to meet Ms Azura and update her on the happenings in the castle. Daniel thanked ma'am and headed toward the dormitory in a scope of escape.

Chapter 8

Nonna desperately dashed a string of complaints,' My lady, when I was watering my plants with affection an elf entered the botany garden playing with a ball. The elf was the guard of room 59. It is important to find out that something strange happened that he is never off his duty'

Ms. Azura desperately replied 'Hmmm. Something is fishy.'

During dinner, Ms Azura called the elf who guarded room 59 and asked him to move around the dining area where everyone was having their dinner and bring her the child who handed over that ball to him.

The elf strolled around the room but couldn't recognise any face that he met outside room 59 as his attention was into playing with the ball.

He returned to Azura alone.

She frustratedly asked, "Who is the culprit of this mischief?"

"I don't remember, Ms.," said the elf, sobbing.

Azura stood up, frowning, and asked the students who had given the elf a ball.

Daniel asked dramatically, "A ball? Why would someone give a ball to an elf?"

Azura ignored him and continued, "The culprit must step forward, or you must face the consequences."

No one came forward. Everyone chattered among themselves. It was a hot topic in the dining room. Leena, Suzan, Daniel, and Tofu acted as if they were not aware of what was happening in the castle.

After enjoying a hearty dinner, they made their

way back to the dormitory for the night. Once there, they changed into their comfortable night jumpers and gathered in a circle. Leena's voice held a note of caution as she reminded them, "The rules are becoming increasingly strict, so we need to be extra careful." The squad nodded in understanding and unfurled the map. The map was aesthetic, showcasing intricate details about the kingdom of Hadarki. Next, Daniel opened the middle page of the third book, revealing a tantalizing clue: a mention of a hexagonal ruby. Leena's eyes darted quickly to her locket, and as she opened it, she found the exact red hexagonal ruby she had been anticipating.

After effortlessly discovering the third clue, they eagerly spent an hour examining the map. Tofu promptly retrieved Volas from the shelf and pulled out the recent map of Elysium, holding it upside down. Strangely, they noticed when they held the map upright it gave all the information of Elysium and when upside down it provided the information of Hadarki. The mystery was unravelling with each passing moment. Their next task was clear - They needed to head to Hadarki and free Leena's butterfly from Hadarki's clutches.

Chapter 9

The next morning the squad thought to take Ms. Azura into their confidence to help them out with the clues to fight against Hadarki.

So, Leena and Suzan went to Ms.. Azura's office to convince her. 'May we come in' asked Suzan.

Azura approves their perMs.ion and lets them in. 'What happened my girls?'

'Ma'am we are very loyal students of yours, and we are here to claim that we were the ones who gave the elf a ball and went into room 59 but for a reason. We have found all the clues of

Hadarki, even the original map from room 59. We need your support,' said Leena.

Azura understood the planning of the students.

'So, you have hit the bull's eye. See, kids, Hadarki is very powerful. She has successfully seized the power of approximately 6 castles, which means that anyone who falls into her trap will become her prey. We must avoid falling into her trap at all costs.' said Azura annoyingly.

Suzan consoled 'Ma'am Leena's butterfly has been trapped. So, to help her we are on this Ms.ion. Could you please be in our plan?'.

'Hmm If you request, I would but on one condition that you will not keep something hidden from me. You have to ask me before any action. Deal?'

Leena out of excitement exclaimed, "Deal. So, could we meet at 9 pm in our dormitory for further planning as Daniel and Tofu are involved too?".

'Fine but don't spread the news of your Ms.ion like a forest fire.' Warned Azura.

When Suzan and Leena left the room, they were over the moon and dashed off to tell Daniel and Tofu about their proceedings.

After dinner time, the squad and Ms Azura

assembled in their dormitory. They sat on the bed around the original map to make strategies to barge into Hadarki's castle and make her butterfly-free.

Azura said, 'Listen, Hadarki has a servant who is clever and helps her by advising her next move. I must say Daniel should go and compliment Hadarki and give her fake suggestions to capture Elysium. Show her that you are on her side as he is very good at acting.' Daniel blushed to certain appreciation.

'Then how will we be able to free Leena's butterfly?' asked Tofu

Azura said 'He has to stay there for at least a week and when he thinks the right time to attack her then he will signal us by any means. We mustn't instantly do all the actions. Haven't you heard slow and study wins the race?'

'Then further proceedings will be done according to the situation. I hope it works?'

'That plan is super!' exclaimed Tofu.

Ms. Azura provided them with a book that listed Hadarki's likes and hates. Azura gave Daniel 7 gems from her bag to give Hadarki 1 gem every day as she likes it and will gain trust in you soon.'

The next day, Suzan, Daniel and Tofu were busy preparing Daniel's bag for his mission whereas Leena was packing food for his travel.

After dinner, Suzan read the book that explained the powers of Hadarki and how we can control it.

The following morning, Daniel got a green signal from Ms. Azura and he was off with his butterfly to Hadarki's castle. Zoop he went.

Chapter 10

Daniel set out on an adventurous journey towards Hadarki's cave. The weather was pleasantly mild as he followed the map through a mysterious jungle. Despite the overwhelming beauty of the surroundings, Daniel couldn't shake off the feeling of nervousness in the pit of his stomach as he traversed the dark, dense forest. A chill crept down his spine, but he pressed on with determination until he finally reached the entrance of the cave.

At the entrance, two imposing guardians stood watch, their alert presence impossible to ignore. As Daniel attempted to enter the cave, one of the guardians stepped forward, blocking his path. In a commanding tone, the guardian demanded, "How dare you trespass Lady Hadarki's Cave? What brings you here?"'

As Daniel approached Hadarki's cave, he couldn't help but feel a sense of foreboding. He knew he had to come up with a convincing reason to enter, so he concocted a fake story about being there for Hadarki's benefit, hoping it would be enough to persuade the other guardian to let him in.

The other guardian disappeared into the cave to convey Daniel's request to Hadarki. From outside, they could hear Hadarki's commanding voice booming, "Enter extruder." This sent shivers down Daniel's spine, filling him with fear.

Remembering the wisdom of Ms. Azura's teachings, Daniel focused on keeping calm in the face of this daunting situation. With a deep breath, he gathered his courage and stepped inside the cave. The darkness enveloped him, relieved only by the faint glow of dim lights scattered throughout the room.

Daniel gazed across the chamber and spotted Hadarki sitting regally upon a shining silver stone that illuminated the otherwise dim room. Her long, voluminous curls cascaded down her back, and she adorned herself with striking black stone jewellery that accentuated her powerful presence. She seemed twice the size of Daniel,

Nervously, Daniel stammered, "M...m...my lady, I present you with this exquisite quartz gem. I am here to offer my protection to this vast cave, shielding it from the potential threat of the Elysium Kingdom."

Hadarki was taken aback by Daniel's unexpected declaration. "Who are you, mister?" she inquired with a note of alarm, her eyes searching his face intently.

"I am Daniel. I have been exiled from the Elysium Kingdom. I have also learned of your formidable power, and I have come to pay homage to you and to offer my assistance in defending against any external threats," Daniel explained confidently, though traces of anxiety lingered in his voice.

Perplexed yet intrigued, Hadarki asked, "Tell me, what do you know of their strategy?"

Daniel replied, 'I can't reveal it in open air and anytime. I request you to arrange a room for my stay for 2 weeks in other to preserve your kingdom and demolish the Elysium Kingdom- your ultimate target.'

"Hmm, you will be confined to this cell so that you do not wander at night. Tomorrow morning, you must meet me here immediately. Do you understand?" the queen replied.

"Yes, Your Lady," Daniel affirmed. Hadarki took the gem and locked the room. As Daniel passed the first test to be able to stay at Hadarki's kingdom, he felt a sense of pride. The room contained only a single flickering bonfire, casting eerie shadows across the walls. Numerous spiderwebs adorned the corners, and ants formed their trails across the floor. The room had an unsettling atmosphere, similar to that of a haunted house.

Daniel, feeling unsettled, pondered his next course of action in the dimly lit room. Despite his weariness, sleep eluded him.

The following morning, Daniel awoke to the jarring sound of a relentless pounding on the door. A stern-looking guard loomed outside, signalling for Daniel to accompany him.

Daniel followed the guard into the grand hall. Seated atop her imposing throne, Hadarki regarded Daniel with a penetrating gaze. 'Before uttering a word, I want to ask you why were you removed from the castle?' asked Hadarki.

Daniel mumbled, 'B...because I greatly praised you and was obsessed with your power.'

Chapter 11

Now go and have your breakfast in that room and reach room 45 with the help of a guard to reveal the secret.' Said Hadarki with a firm.

Daniel followed her instructions. He went into the room to have breakfast. He saw many servants eating there. Daniel sat next to the servant who acted as a wise man in the castle. It was a coincidence.

The wise man asked, 'I am Ben, nice to meet you. What brings you to the castle?'

Daniel took the conversation ahead' I am Daniel. I am here to protect this kingdom from the threat of Elysium,

Ben gave him a suspicious look and went away. When Daniel finished munching the tasteless food provided he chucked in a toffee which he had brought for backup.

He sought the assistance of a guard to navigate to the designated room, where he found Hadarki patiently awaiting his arrival. Without hesitation, Daniel placed another gemstone in front of her and uttered, "My honour." Hadarki's voice was stern as she inquired, "So, tell me the strategy." Daniel's response was filled with confidence as he stated, "Yes, the time has come for revelation, my lady. A magnificent butterfly, possessing the power to infiltrate the cave, has come to my attention. The attack is scheduled for either this week or the next. The ball is now in your court, whether to trust me or not." To Daniel's delight, Hadarki disclosed, "We have managed to capture a butterfly from the Elysium kingdom. Would you care to have a look?" Euphoria washed over Daniel as Hadarki led the way to the room, marking another achievement.

Exiting the eerie cave, they ventured into the jungle, where the echoes of bats filled the air. The path was haunting, with trees drooping and shedding their leaves. After a five-minute trek through the jungle, they arrived at the pitch-black cave where not a single flame burned. Hadarki swiftly ignited a fire by rubbing two stones together, casting light into the cave. There, a pitiful butterfly lay on the ground, exhausted and defeated, its wings tattered and soiled. Hadarki let out a chilling laughter, remarking, "Hahahaha!! Look at this wretched creature. Doesn't it look endearing in this state?" Daniel meekly nodded under the oppressive gaze of Hadarki.

Upon their return to the castle, Daniel retreated to his chambers while Hadarki retired to her own. A wise servant knocked on the door, but Hadarki flung it open and snapped, "My Lady, please do not heed Daniel's words. It is a trap. He merely seeks to extract our secrets." Annoyed, Hadarki responded, "I know what I am doing. Do not attempt to meddle in our affairs."

'But, try to understand the depth, my Lady. 'Ben tried to convince Hadarki. 'If you argue with me one more time I will remove you from the castle.'

Ben went out desperately.

Meanwhile, in the Elysium Kingdom, Ms Azura, Leena, Suzan, and Tofu eagerly awaited Daniel's signals.

Chapter 12

It was dinner time. Hadarki's door was left ajar, so Daniel seized the opportunity to slip into her room and surreptitiously poured a few drops of poison into her food while she went to her throne to get her crown. As he was exiting Hadarki's chamber, Hadarki spotted him going out and quickly stopped him. "Stop right there, young man.

Why did you come into this room? What are you up

to?" she asked suspiciously, her brow furrowed.

Daniel quickly responded, "Oh, my Lady, I've been looking for you. I called out for you from outside for the past five minutes, but when I got no response, I thought I'd go back to my dormitory." Hadarki demanded, "Why were you calling me?" Daniel hesitantly replied, "I wanted to give you these five gems." Hadarki ordered him, "Hand them over and then go have your dinner.

After a brief handover, Daniel made his way

straight to the dining room where he joined Ben. Ben seemed to pay little attention to him, preoccupied with his plans in the kingdom and even leading Hadarki astray. Initiating the conversation, Daniel asked, "Hey, how's it going? How long have you been working in this kingdom?" Ben responded with "5 years" before promptly leaving.

Following dinner, Daniel also returned to his dormitory, secretly hoping that Hadarki would suffer from food poisoning.

That's what exactly happened, she became incredibly nauseous and was bedridden with a high fever. The following morning, when he arrived at Hadarki's throne, she was nowhere to be found. He proceeded to Hadarki's chamber and gently knocked on the door. Hadarki's hoarse voice croaked out the command to enter.

Daniel walked into the room and was taken aback by the sight of Hadarki's pale face. Concerned, he asked, "My Lady, what happened? You look unwell." Hadarki responded, "I have food poisoning. Someone foolishly poisoned my food, and I am determined to find out who did it. Please, go and fetch Ben for me." Daniel quickly sought out

Ben, urging him to go to Hadarki's room right away, as she needed to speak with him. Ben hurried to her room and anxiously inquired, "You called me, my Lady. What has happened to you?"

Hadarki's long, sharp nails grew rapidly, a telltale sign of her mounting anger. She pointed accusatory fingers, her voice laced with venom, "Food poisoning. All because of you. I'm certain it's your doing. Your jealousy towards Daniel has been evident since yesterday. You're fired. No more warnings. I hope this is clear to you."

Ben's words were barely audible as he mumbled and solemnly said, 'B...but it is not my mischief.' Hadarki, filled with rage, shouted, "Stop, Ben!" The guards were ordered to return his belongings and escort him outside the castle. Ben felt hopeless and frustrated with the situation, especially with Daniel.

Meanwhile, Daniel was filled with glee as he successfully removed the wise person from the cave, making his task much easier with fewer obstacles to face. He was well-prepared with the cure and requested Hadarki to administer it. The next morning, Hadarki was energetic and had completely recovered from her illness.

Daniel's actions instilled a sense of trust in Hadarki, as she realized the sincerity and care behind his intentions.

Chapter 13

Daniel, taking advantage of the unique opportunity, approached Hadarki with a sense of curiosity and asked, "May I have the liberty to traverse this fascinating place and explore its hidden gems?" Responded with a gracious smile, "Absolutely! why don't I arrange for a guard to accompany you, guiding you through the intricate pathways and secrets of this place?"

Without a moment's hesitation, Daniel replied, "Thank you, but I prefer to venture into the unknown on my own."

Agreeing to Daniel's request, Hadarki nodded, watching as Daniel veiled his swift departure with the illusion of exploring the surroundings. Little did anyone know that, in reality, Daniel had vanished with breathtaking speed, making his way to Elysium unnoticed.

Leena spotted him. She waved him in the sky. He took a soft landing. He was proud to tell the current happenings to them.

Leena paced long steps to gather Ms.Azura, Suzan and Tofu.

Daniel said, 'I give you the green signal, to come there. Just hint me whenever you reach there through any means so that I can distract her. I am short of time. Hoping to see you soon.'

Before Ms.Azura uttered a word, Daniel fled away.

Daniel reached Hadarki's kingdom as soon as possible. Hadarki questioned, 'What took you so long?'

'Nothing' replied Daniel insanely. He handed her 10 gems again.

The following morning he received a letter that highly praised Hadarki and the message had a code hidden in it.

It was written by Leena mentioning that they would arrive by 1 pm and asked him to tell her the location of her butterfly.

Daniel, using his quick wit, devised a plan and strategically placed red butterfly stickers along a trail leading to a hidden cave. In response to a letter, he opted to communicate using a coded language, guiding the recipient to follow the trail marked by the red butterflies. After some time, to Daniel's surprise, Hadarki entered his chamber. Reacting swiftly, Daniel stood and inquired, "What's the matter? Why are you here? You could have simply called me."

In a fit of deep-seated anger, Hadarki questioned, "Why did you place those red butterfly stickers on the trail?"

Defending himself, Daniel mumbled, "I have a tendency to forget things, so I used the stickers to mark the area for convenience."

With a pensive "Hmm," Hadarki left the room. Concurrently, Ms Azura and her squad were on a mission to rescue Leena's butterfly. Azura instructed her team to target the gem on Hadarki's crown, which served as the source of her power. Venturing into the ominous dark forest, they diligently followed the trail of red butterflies, with Tofu leading the way. Eventually, they stealthily reached the cave without raising any alarms.

Chapter 14

The sight of the butterfly was merciful. It was on the verge of death, its power was taken away from it and stored in a crystal ball.

Tofu noticed a rusted lock hanging from the chain that held Leena's delicate butterfly. He called everyone over, wanting them to see it too. Suzan's eyes lit up as she blurted out, "The lock's intricate design looks exactly like the one on Leena's locket!" Leena was abashed when she realized the truth of

Suzan's observation. Without a moment to spare, she took off her locket from her neck and used it to unlock the chain. But as soon as the lock clicked open, the door slammed shut, trapping them inside. Panic set in as Suzan exclaimed "Regardo!" She uttered a spell and illuminated the room with her wand. The eerie light revealed their surroundings, and they all frantically searched for a way to escape.

Daniel, wanted to inquire if they had gone to look for Leena's butterfly. Daniel received permission from Hadarki to go outside. When he arrived there, he heard the cries and shrill calls of his squad.

Daniel promptly sprang into action and reassured them, saying, "Stay calm, I'm on my way to rescue you."

He then approached Hadarki and presented her with five gems, asking, "Your Highness, is there any alternative route to reach the cave where the butterfly is trapped? I left my wand there. Moreover, I'm feeling a bit apprehensive about the weather outside."

Hadarki had a sensation of unease, a feeling that something was mischievous. She responded cunningly, "Yes, I will guide you on the path, but only if you allow me to come with you. Will you agree to that?" Daniel was initially taken aback by the idea of being responsible for saving his friends' lives, but he realized that he had no choice and nodded in agreement. Hadarki took the lead and began to reveal the secret passage to him. The passage, concealed within her room, extended through the very walls of her kingdom. She uttered something under her breath as they reached the entrance, causing the gate to open without a sound.

A cold chill ran down Daniel's spine. As Hadarki flung the door open, everyone was shocked to see her there. Hadarki screamed 'Sister! You are here finally in my hands. What a luck! the devil itself came for its fate. Ha! Ha! Ha!' pointing Azura. Leena couldn't handle the cruelty any longer. With a fierce determination burning in her eyes, she attempted to unleash the powerful spell 'Kandamo' at Hadarki, but her aim faltered, causing the spell to miss its target. As Hadarki prepared to strike back, Tofu sprang into action, using her immense strength to shield Leena with a colossal stone, creating a protective barrier amidst the chaos.

In a quiet but urgent whisper, Suzan directed Leena to focus her attack on Hadarki's forehead, the one vulnerable spot she could exploit. Meanwhile, Azura fought valiantly but struggled to gain the upper hand against Hadarki. Suddenly, the door flew open, Ben stormed in and joined the fray with fierce attacks aimed primarily at Daniel.

Amid the uproar, Leena instinctively took a step back, distancing herself from the ongoing battle. With Suzan's guidance echoing in her ears, she focused on Hadarki's forehead. Gathering her strength, Leena shouted the spell 'Quosi' and defeated Hadarki. As soon as they got the victory, Hadarki and Ben lost, and the kingdom started falling off. Hadarki's once grandiose kingdom crumbled into oblivion, with chunks of rock and crystal falling from the ceiling, creating a chaotic cascade of debris It felt as if it rained stones. Hadarki lowered her wand realizing what happened to her kingdom and Azura quickly attacked her with her spell and took her within her control.

As they fled from the oppressive darkness of the

cave, Leena's fragile butterfly fluttered weakly but then found the determination to break free. With swift agility, everyone mounted their butterflies and fled, leaving Hadarki to fend for herself in the depths of the kingdom. As they emerged into the open air, Suzan couldn't help but exclaim, "Magnificent!" It was at that moment that Leena realized her special connection with her butterfly, which revealed its extraordinary power of light. The radiant glow emanating from the butterfly illuminated their path, guiding them safely through the dark forest until they were finally free.

Chapter 15

The gang felt elated after successfully saving the butterfly. They returned to the place of Elysium. Everyone waited eagerly for their arrival. They organized a grand fest as they were able to demolish the evil. The queens and kings of other kingdoms who were under her control of Hadarki joined the fest to thank them.

Leena's locket started to shine again. Azura said it was because her parents eagerly awaited her on the land. So Leena recited a lullaby to her dearest butterfly before leaving:

In the gentle embrace of the evening breeze, my dear,

I weave tender words, though bittersweet emotions swell within.

Your vibrant wings, adorned with hues of gold and glitter,

Now sway gracefully among the shimmering stars in the tranquil night sky.

The paths ahead may twist and wind,

Yet in our hearts, the ties that bind.

Each memory we've crafted will softly play,

In the symphony of life, come what may.

Each moment we shared is now a cherished memory,

Though our paths may diverge, your finding seems to be finding a treasury,

Though distance may stretch like the vast, open sea,

Know that a piece of you will always be with me.

Farewell for now, but not a final goodbye,

In every whispered breeze and soft sigh of the

sky,

You will forever hold a luminous place in my heart,

My dearest butterfly, embrace your journey and take flight.

Later Ms. Azura rewarded her with the most powerful gem and she permitted Leena to visit the castle whenever she wished to. Azura made arrangements for her back home. Before going Leena whispered a few words in Azura's ear and waved her friends goodbye. The butterfly flew aloft to leave her safely to her parents.

The
End

www.ingramcontent.com/pod-product-compliance
Lightning Source LLC
LaVergne TN
LVHW041231150826
845673LV00008B/2351

* 9 7 9 8 8 9 6 7 3 6 9 1 2 *